Oddly Colorful

by Brenda Baker

illustrated by Maia Batumashvili

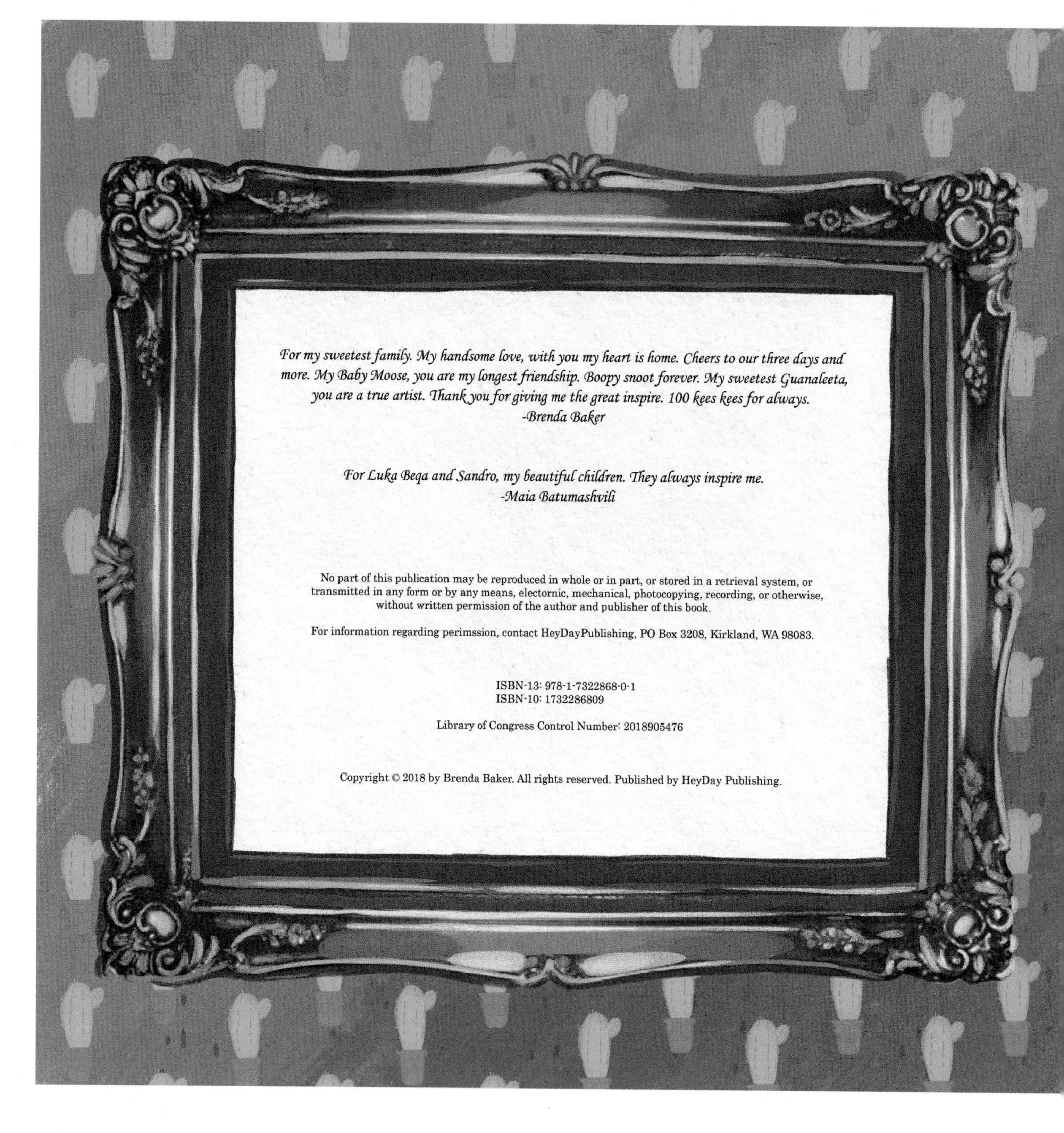

For my sweetest family. My handsome love, with you my heart is home. Cheers to our three days and more. My Baby Moose, you are my longest friendship. Boopy snoot forever. My sweetest Guanaleeta, you are a true artist. Thank you for giving me the great inspire. 100 kees kees for always.
-Brenda Baker

For Luka Beqa and Sandro, my beautiful children. They always inspire me.
-Maia Batumashvili

For information regarding perimssion, contact HeyDayPublishing, PO Box 3208, Kirkland, WA 98083.

ISBN-13: 978-1-7322868-0-1
ISBN-10: 1732286809

Library of Congress Control Number: 2018905476

Darren is an odd boy.

He likes to paint with mud, not watercolor.

He likes to sleep upside down in his bed and brush his teeth
with two toothbrushes at once.

For his birthday he wanted a carrot cake. So, his dad made him a moist and beautiful carrot cake with fluffy white frosting.

“No,” Darren insisted, “not a cake like that. Just carrots.
In a circle so they look like a cake.”
Odd.

At the playground, Darren climbs
under the slide and looks for
misplaced snails.

One day someone asked him, “Why are you so odd?”
“I’m just being myself!” smiled Darren.

Walking to school
on his hands
instead of his feet,
collecting buttons
that only have
two polka dots,

teaching himself to play guitar
with his big toe.

Odd, odd, odd.

One day, on an ordinary Tuesday morning,
a moving truck stopped right next to
Darren's house.

And out walked
Linda Lee-Ta-Da-Look-At-Me.

On her hands,
of course.

"Hi!" Darren stuck out his foot. "I'm Darren. Who are you?"

"I'm Linda Lee Ta-Da-Look-At-Me," and she stuck her foot right back at him.

Darren grinned. “I have a polka dot button collection, you know.” Linda Lee was shocked!

"I have a shirt collection, but they don't have any buttons!" Linda Lee announced proudly.

"I like to peel the frosting off of cupcakes and make snowmen sculptures out of them," declared Linda Lee Ta-Da-Look-At-Me. "Then I put them in the freezer until the snowy season when they can be released back into the wild."

"Wow..." was all Darren could say.

"Some people think I'm odd," Darren whispered to Linda Lee.

"Some people are too plain to think colorful thoughts," whispered Linda Lee right back to him.

“I like colorful thoughts! I like noodles for breakfast and tissue paper necklaces and socks with holes in them so my toes can see the world!” shouted Darren.

Linda Lee sat on the ground. She kicked off her shoes and showed her toes to the world, too.

"Wow..." was all she could say.

They sat on the curb with their hands on their heads
and their toes to the sky.

They stayed like that for a long while.

Someone walked by and snickered, “You two are odd.”
Darren and Linda Lee Ta-Da-Look-At-Me giggled quietly.

“Some people don’t understand. Maybe they’re too afraid to show their insides on their outsides...” Darren pondered out loud.

"They should be brave, in spite of themselves," nodded Linda Lee. "Because everybody's odd one way or another!"

“It’s good to be colorful,
I’m the first one you’ll see
in a crowd!” agreed Linda
Lee Ta-Da-Look-At-Me.

“It’s good to be odd,
people never forget me!”
laughed Darren.

Darren is an odd boy.

And Linda Lee Ta-Da-Look-At-Me is an odd girl.

And that's just fine with them, they like it that way!
They're happy about who they are.

And together, with their odd and colorful insides
on their outsides, they head down the road
in search of new adventures.

Keeping an eye out for misplaced snails, of course.

Made in the USA
Lexington, KY
26 October 2018